FRACTURED FAIRY TALES

THE LITTLE MERMAID'S SONG

Graphic Planet

An Imprint of Magic Wagon
abdobooks.com

THIS BOOK IS DEDICATED TO THE GASHLER FAMILY: MIKE, DESIRE, JAMIE, TALIA, AND EVAN!
LOVE IS LOVE. -AM

TO MY SON HEITOR, WHO LOVES WHAT I DO. AND TO MY WIFE JO, WHO WAS WITH ME UNTIL LATE AT NIGHT WHILE I ILLUSTRATED THIS BOOK. LOVE YOU GUYS. -LA

abdobooks.com

Published by Magic Wagon, a division of ABDO, PO Box 398166, Minneapolis, Minnesota 55439. Copyright © 2021 by Abdo Consulting Group, Inc. International copyrights reserved in all countries.
No part of this book may be reproduced in any form without written permission from the publisher. Graphic Planet™ is a trademark and logo of Magic Wagon.

Printed in the United States of America, North Mankato, Minnesota.
102020
012021

 THIS BOOK CONTAINS
RECYCLED MATERIALS

Written by Andy Mangels
Illustrated and Colored by Lelo Alves
Lettered by Kathryn S. Renta
Editorial supervision by David Campiti/MJ Macedo
Packaged by Glass House Graphics
Art Directed by Candice Keimig
Editorial Support by Bridget O'Brien

Library of Congress Control Number: 2020941556

Publisher's Cataloging-in-Publication Data

Names: Mangels, Andy, author. | Alves, Lelo, illustrator.
Title: The little mermaid's song / by Andy Mangels ; illustrated by Lelo Alves.
Description: Minneapolis, Minnesota : Magic Wagon, 2021. | Series: Fractured fairy tales
Summary: Marilla must make a choice between trying out for a singing competition with her new friend and competing in a big swim meet to make her parents proud.
Identifiers: ISBN 9781532139758 (lib. bdg.) ISBN 9781098230036 (ebook) | ISBN 9781098230173 (Read-to-Me ebook)
Subjects: LCSH: Singing--Juvenile fiction. | Parent and child--Juvenile fiction. | Swim teams--Juvenile fiction. | Fairy tales--Juvenile fiction. | Friendship--Juvenile fiction. | Graphic novels--Juvenile fiction.
Classification: DDC 741.5--dc23

TABLE OF CONTENTS

4

HOW COME YOU CAN'T SWIM?

THEY DIDN'T HAVE A LOT OF SWIMMING POOLS WHERE I GREW UP.

TAKEN TO RESCUING KIDS IN TROUBLE, MARILLA?

ONLY WHEN THEY NEED IT, HALI.

GOOD. YOU'LL NEED SOME KIND OF SKILLS TO FALL BACK ON. THEY CAN ALWAYS USE MORE LIFEGUARDS AT THE COMMUNITY POOL.

MAYBE YOU CAN GIVE DENYS SOME LESSONS SINCE WINNING THE REGIONALS ISN'T IN YOUR FUTURE.

I DON'T NEED ANY LESSONS. I JUST NEED TO GET EXCUSED FROM GYM CLASS.

It's strange how bullies can make us feel so bad about ourselves...

My dad says that "hurt people hurt others," but why do they have to hurt anyone?

Why can't they just look for support instead?

YOU SING REALLY GOOD, TOO.

"WELL." YOU SING REALLY "WELL."

WHATEVER, LOL.

I'M SERIOUS! AND WE SOUNDED GREAT TOGETHER.

THIS COULD BE WHAT YOU "FALL BACK" ON.

OH YEAH, WE'RE DESTINED FOR GREATNESS.

TWO STARS ARE BORN!

WAIT! I'VE GOT AN IDEA. YOU NEED TO LEARN HOW TO SWIM, RIGHT?

WELL, I GUESS SO...

SO, I'LL TRADE YOU. SWIM LESSONS, FOR SINGING WITH ME.

WE HAVE A DEAL?

NOW THEY WANT YOU TO COME OVER AND HAVE DINNER.

GO KRAKENS

IT'S NOT LIKE WE'RE DATING!

I KNOW, RIGHT. APPARENTLY, IN THEIR DAY, BOYS AND GIRLS COULDN'T JUST BE FRIENDS.

HEY, LOOK AT THAT!

YOUNG STARZ 2

YOUNG STARZ 2

WHOAAAAH!

DO YOU WANNA DO IT?

I DON'T KNOW... DO YOU THINK WE'RE GOOD ENOUGH?

YOU TWO THINKING OF AUDITIONING? IT'S A PRETTY BIG DEAL.

I KNOW BECAUSE MY UNCLE IS ONE OF THE PRODUCERS.

SERIOUSLY? LIKE A "PRODUCER" PRODUCER?

DUH.

HE'S IN CHARGE OF EVERYTHING. LIKE, WHO GETS TO AUDITION, WHO GETS TO THE FINALS, WHO GOES TO HOLLYWOOD.

I INTERNED WITH HIM LAST YEAR. IT WAS COOL, I GUESS...

...IF THAT SORT OF THING IS IMPORTANT TO YOU.

THAT WAS REALLY LOVELY, MARILLA! I HAD NO IDEA YOU WERE SO TALENTED.

THAT'S MY BOY! HE'S GONNA BE A STAR!

MOMMMMF!

OMG MARILLA, THAT WAS AWESOME!

SOOOO CLUTCH!

ARE YOU GONNA TRY OUT FOR YOUNG STARZ?

I DON'T KNOW. WE'RE THINKING ABOUT IT.

I THINK YOU SHOULD DO IT.

YOU'VE BOTH GOT TALENT.

UMMM, THANKS. BUT WE'D HAVE TO GET INTO THE AUDITIONS...

I CAN'T BELIEVE WE GOT HERE AT 5 IN THE MORNING AND WE'RE STILL SO FAR BACK IN LINE.

AND THIS IS JUST THE LINE TO GET AN AUDITION TIME SLOT, NOT EVEN THE AUDITIONS THEMSELVES!

WE SHOULD HAVE BROUGHT FOLDING CHAIRS.

I WONDER HOW MANY PEOPLE THEY'RE TAKING?

I DON'T KNOW. IT JUST SAID "LIMITED" ON THE POSTER.

YOU WANT A SANDWICH?

NO. MY STOMACH'S IN KNOTS ALREADY.

HEY, IT LOOKS LIKE THEY'RE GOING TO ANNOUNCE SOMETHING!

YEAH. MINE, TOO. I JUST NEED SOMETHING TO DO WITH MY HANDS.

... AND REMEMBER THAT NO MATTER WHO WINS, EVERYONE HAS TRIED THEIR BEST. THEY'VE BEEN TRAINING JUST LIKE WE HAVE.

BE GRACIOUS, COMPLIMENT THEM, AND SHAKE THEIR HANDS.

THAT SAID, THE MERMAIDS ARE GONNA WIN! GO MERMAIDS!

HEY, HOW ARE YOU FEELING ABOUT TODAY?

YOU MEAN ABOUT YOUR OFFER?

DID I MAKE AN OFFER? I DON'T THINK I DID.

I JUST TOLD YOU THAT I NEED TO WIN TODAY.

AND I TOLD YOU THAT I COULD HELP YOU... IF I WANT TO.

YEAH, YOU'RE REALLY SUBTLE.

YOU THINK THAT BECAUSE I DIDN'T GET INTO THE AUDITIONS THAT I'M GOING TO LET YOU WIN.

BUT I'M NOT.

IF IT MEANS I DON'T GET TO AUDITION, THEN IT ISN'T MY TIME.

IF YOU WANT TO WIN, YOU'RE GOING TO HAVE TO BEAT ME.

FAIR AND SQUARE.

EARN IT, HALI.

THAT'S THE RIGHT WAY TO GET WHAT YOU WANT.

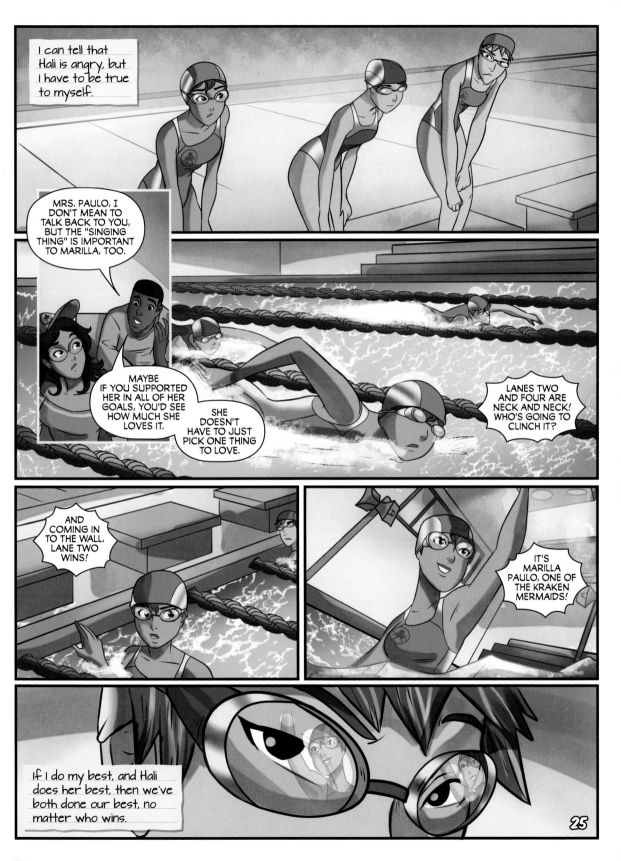

LATER...

HEY, MARILLA, WAIT UP.

CONGRATULATIONS ON WINNING TODAY.

REALLY?

I MEAN IT THIS TIME.

AND THANKS FOR SENDING TREADMAN MY WAY, AND FOR WHAT YOU SAID. YOU DIDN'T HAVE TO BE NICE.

THEY'RE KEEPING ME ON THEIR RADAR AND INVITED ME UP TO SEE THE SCHOOL!

I HAVE SOMETHING FOR YOU, TOO. A TICKET FOR THE LAST AUDITION SPOT.

BUT I THOUGHT YOU'D BE...

GRATEFUL? YOU MADE ME SO MAD I PUSHED MYSELF HARDER THAN EVER. AND I DID BEAT MY BEST TIME.

THANK YOU!

GO AUDITION. AND WIN IT, FAIR AND SQUARE!

I CAN'T BELIEVE HALI DID THE RIGHT THING!

I GUESS SHE SAW THAT PLAYING BY THE RULES IS ALWAYS BEST, EVEN IF IT ISN'T EASY.

NOW, WE'VE GOT A LOT OF PRACTICING TO DO IF WE'RE GOING TO SING OUR WAY TO HOLLYWOOD!

...THE END... FOR NOW!

29

WHAT DO YOU THINK?

WHEN YOU REALLY WANT SOMETHING, AND YOU WORK OR STUDY OR PRACTICE HARD TO GET IT, YOU'RE WORKING TOWARD YOUR GOALS! BUT THERE ARE OFTEN OTHER PEOPLE WHO ARE ALSO WORKING TOWARD THE SAME GOALS. YOU CAN TRY YOUR BEST, BUT IT'S IMPORTANT TO BE FAIR TO OTHERS WHO ARE TRYING THEIR BEST AS WELL. CHEATERS WHO LOOK FOR AN EASY WAY TO WIN RARELY GET WHAT THEY WANT IN THE END. STAYING TRUE TO YOUR GOALS AND WORKING TO ACHIEVE THEM IS THE BEST WAY TO WIN.

- Marilla makes a trade with Denys and shared her talent in exchange for him sharing his. Have you ever made a deal with someone to help you with something and you would help them? Did you feel like that was a business deal, or was it fun to share?

- On the opposite side, Hali makes an offer to Marilla to let her win the swim meet, and Hali will get Marilla the audition she wants. Have you ever had someone offer to do something for you that you want, in exchange for you doing something you didn't want to do? How did you react?

- Marilla's mom wants her to concentrate on school and swimming and doesn't support her goals. But she's not being mean. She just wants Marilla to excel in areas she's good at. Her mom grows by seeing that Marilla can handle several things at once. Are there things you want to do that you wish you had more support to do?

- Denys and Marilla have decided to just be friends, even though their parents think there's a romance between them. Good friendship is important. Do you have friends that are just friends that people think you have a romantic interest in? How do you tell people that you're "just friends" without making them sound like they're not important?

- At her birthday party, Marilla made a choice to sing in front of friends and family, which was brave. What's the bravest thing you've done? Were you still worried after it was over, or were you glad you did it?

NEW STORIES & OLD TALES:
FAIRY TALE FUN FACTS

1. Although the term "Fairy Tale" was translated from a French collection by Madame D'Aulnoy in 1697, fairy tales have been around since people could talk and write. They generally include magical beings and often have rivalries between two characters.

2. Hans Christian Anderson's "The Little Mermaid" was first published in 1837 as part of a collection of Danish fairy tales. It is about a young mermaid who gives up her life underwater in order to become human. She visits a Sea Witch who gives her a potion to become human in exchange for her voice. The beloved story has been adapted for opera, ballet, stage plays, musicals, film, television, animation, and toys.

3. There are three statues of the Little Mermaid in Italy and one in the country of Monaco. The most famous statue is on a rock in a harbor of Copenhagen, Denmark.

4. The most famous adaptation of Anderson's "The Little Mermaid" is the 1989 Disney film of the same name. It won two Academy Awards, and was later made into a live Broadway musical. It led to the name Ariel becoming one of the most popular names for little girls for several years.

5. Mermaids have appeared in folk tales and fairy tales since before written language! They are almost always beautiful women, whose lower body is a fish tail. They almost always sing beautifully and were said to lure sailors to shipwreck or other disasters. Some people think mermaids are a type of sea creature called a manatee, but others still believe that mermaids swim the ocean today!

GLOSSARY

AUDITION — To give a trial performance showcasing personal talent as a musician, a singer, a dancer, or an actor.

COMPETITION — A contest between two or more persons or groups.

GOALS — Something that a person works to reach or complete.

HARMONIES — The playing of musical tones together in chords. Also a pleasing arrangement of parts.

INTERN — An intern is a student or somebody in training gaining guided practice experience in a professional field.

MEDLEY — A varied mixture of people or things.

RECRUIT — To get someone to join a group. A person who recruits people is called a recruiter.

SCOUT — Someone sent to discover new talented athletes or entertainers.

ONLINE RESOURCES

Booklinks
NONFICTION NETWORK
FREE! ONLINE NONFICTION RESOURCES

To learn more about FAIRY TALES, GOALS, and COMPETITION, please visit abdobooklinks.com or scan this QR code. These links are routinely monitored and updated to provide the most current information available.